HOW TO DRAW
CARTOONS

Judy Tatchell
Designed by Graham Round
Illustrated by Graham Round, Terry Bave, Robert Walster
and Chris Lyon

Revised by Anna Milbourne and Mairi Mackinnon
Cover design by Russell Punter
Cover illustration by Christyan Fox

Additional designs by Brian Robertson and Camilla Luff
With thanks to Katarina Dragoslavić

AF469141

CONTENTS

About this book

Cartoons look quick and easy to draw. You may have found that they are not as easy as they look, though. This book is full of simple ways to draw good cartoons.

The first part tells you how to draw cartoon people using simple shapes and lines. You can find out how to draw expressions and show movement, too.

You can also use cartoon techniques to draw caricatures. A caricature is a funny picture of a real person. To draw them, you exaggerate things, such as the shape of their nose or hair.

A comic strip, sometimes called a strip cartoon, is a series of pictures which tell a joke or funny short story. You can find out how to build up your own comic strips on pages 16-19.

You might find one or more longer cartoon stories in a comic book. Some comic books feature characters, such as Asterix and Tintin, that are popular all around the world.

Cartoons can also be made into films for cinema or television. Cartoon films are called animation, which means "the giving of life". Cartoons are brought to life in a film.

Learn about line and shape, the basic elements of drawing, with Carmine the Chameleon at ***www.Sanford-artadventures.com/play/lineshape/flash3page-html.***

First faces

This page shows you an easy way to draw cartoon faces. All you need is a pencil and a sheet of paper. If you want to colour the faces in, you can use coloured pencils or felt-tip pens.

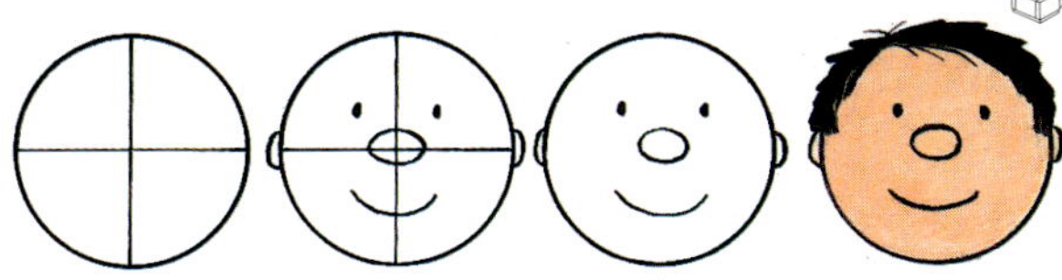

Draw a circle. Do two pencil lines crossing it. Put the nose where the lines cross. The ears are level with the nose.

The eyes go slightly above the nose. Rub out the lines crossing the face. Add any sort of hair you like, then colour the face.

Faces to copy

Here are some more faces for you to copy. You can see how in a cartoon some things are exaggerated, such as the size of the nose or the expression.

Looking around

Draw these lines in pencil so you can rub them out later.

Nose goes where lines cross

Ear moves round

As the face turns more, this line moves further round.

Profile

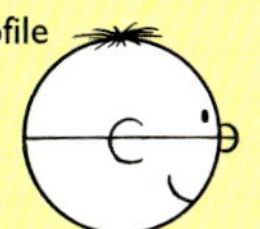

The first picture shows a face from the front, with lines crossing it. As the face looks to the side, the line going across the face stays where it is. The line going down curves to one side. The curve of the line makes the head look ball-shaped.

This is a side view, or profile. Draw a line across the middle of the head to show you where the nose and ears go.

Line curves up in the middle

The more the face tilts upward, the more the line curves.

Line curves down in the middle

To draw a face looking up, do a line across the face as shown. The nose goes in the centre and the ears at each end of the line.

For a face looking down, the line curves down in the middle. Can you see how the face looking up and to one side is drawn?

You can use any of the pictures marked with this symbol as clip art on your computer. To download them, go to ***www.usborne-quicklinks.com***

Cartoon people

Now you can try adding some bodies to your cartoon faces. There are two different methods described on these pages. The first uses stick figures. The second uses rounded shapes. Try them both and see which you find easier.

Stick figures

Draw this stick figure. The body stick is slightly longer than the head. The legs are slightly longer than the body. The arms are a little shorter than the legs.

Here are the outlines of some clothes for the figure. You can copy a sweatshirt with jeans or with a skirt. You could also try some dungarees or a dress.

To dress your stick figure, draw the clothes round it, starting at the neck and working down. You can add long, short, curly or straight hair.

Drawing hands and feet

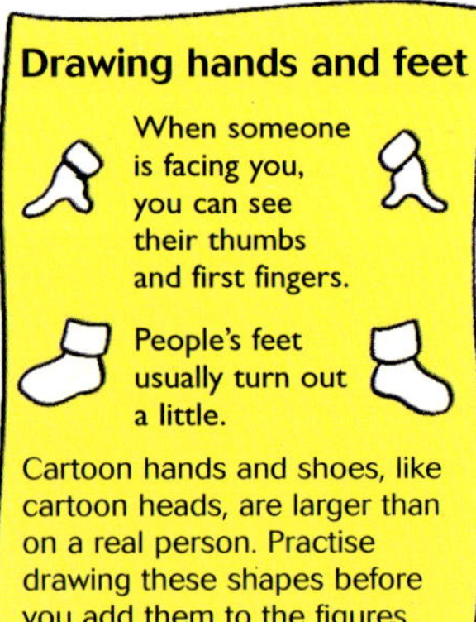

Cartoon hands and shoes, like cartoon heads, are larger than on a real person. Practise drawing these shapes before you add them to the figures.

Colouring in

When you have finished the outline of the figure, go over it with a felt-tip. Once it is dry you can rub the stick figure out and colour the cartoon.

The girl needs some lines for her legs before you can add her shoes. When you colour the shoes, leave a small white patch on the toes to make them shiny.

Figures using rounded shapes

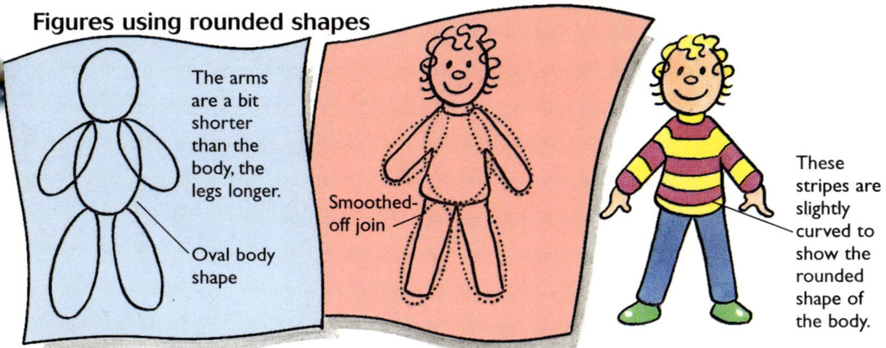

With a pencil, draw a head shape. Add an oval for the body shape and sausages for the arms and legs. The body is about one and a half times as long as the head.

Add the outlines of the clothes, smoothing off any joins, such as between the arms or legs and the body. Go over the outline in pen and rub out pencil lines.

Add hands and feet and colour the figure in. You can find out how to make your cartoon figure look as though it is moving on pages 10-11.

More cartoon people to draw

Try varying your rounded shapes or stick figures to draw all sorts of different-shaped cartoon people.

Tiny person – head larger in proportion to body

Tall person – egg-shaped head and longer body

Fat person – squashed head and shorter legs

Short person – head, body and legs the same length

Some things to try

When you have practised drawing several figures using the methods shown above, you could try drawing a figure outline straight away. If you find it difficult, you can go back to drawing a stick or a rounded shape figure first.

Try drawing all these different people:

- A fat lady wearing a fur coat and hat
- A man with hairy legs wearing shorts
- A boy and a girl in their party clothes.

Making faces

You can make cartoon characters come to life by giving them different expressions. These two pages show you how to do this, by adding or changing a few lines.

First, try drawing the faces in pencil. Then you can colour them in.

Happy faces

Girls and women tend to have slightly smaller noses than boys and men.

These lines make the ears look more real.

Happiness is shown by drawing a smiling mouth. Drawing the eyes as shown above gives a cheerful expression.

You can make the person burst out laughing by opening the mouth more and showing the teeth.

This is a bigger laugh. The head is thrown back. You can find out how to position the features on page 3.

Sad and angry faces

Sadness and anger are also mainly shown in the eyes and mouth.

Lines show shaking with fury.

Sad: the mouth and eyebrows droop.

Angry: use straight lines for the mouth and eyebrows.

Furious: the person frowns and goes red in the face.

Hopping mad: the mouth is wide open in a loud yell.

See lots more ways to draw different expressions at
www.cartooncorner.com/artsfolder/howtacartoon/cartooning.html

More expressions

Here are lots more faces for you to practise. You can add bodies in different positions.

Remember that a person's head might be facing you while the body is sideways.

White stripes in hair make it look shiny.

Smug: sideways grin and half-closed eyes.

Winking: mouth tilts up on side while eye is closed.

You can make the face look fatter by adding curves on the cheeks and chin.

Girls' and boys' faces are similar shapes but they can have different hairstyles.

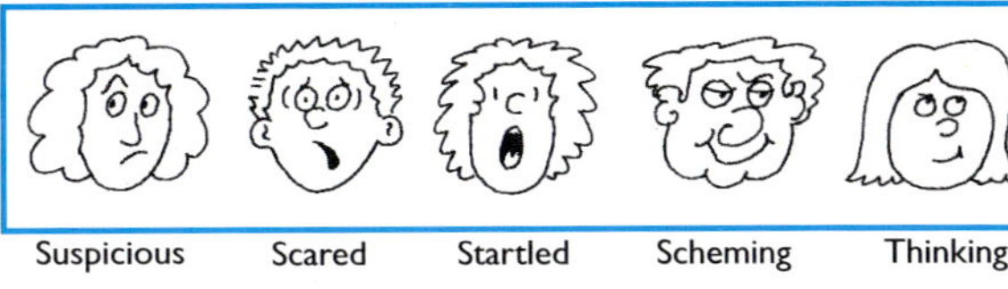

Suspicious Scared Startled Scheming Thinking

Happy Laughing Sad Angry Crying

Spiky hair Long hair Plaited hair Balding head Woolly hat

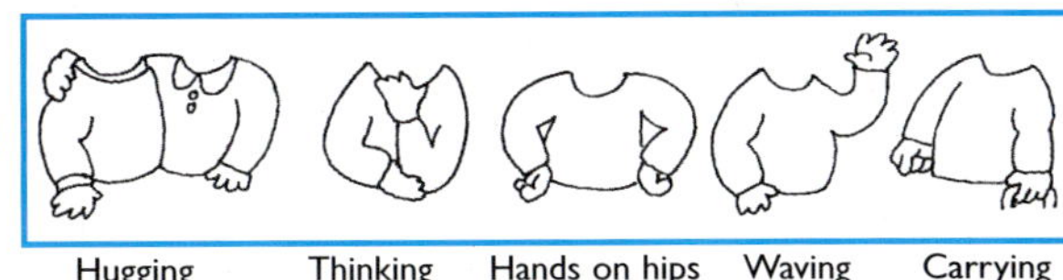

Hugging Thinking Hands on hips Waving Carrying

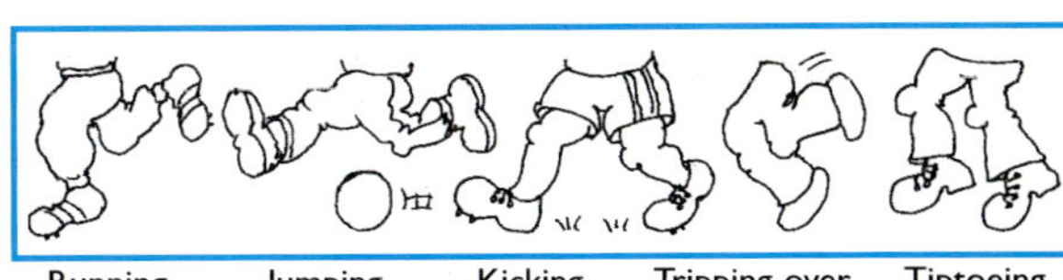

Running Jumping Kicking Tripping over Tiptoeing

Drawing from different sides

Here you can find out how to draw people from the side and from the back as well as from the front. You can also see how to make your pictures more interesting by drawing a bird's-eye view (looking down) or a worm's-eye view (looking up). There are some instructions to help you do this on the opposite page.

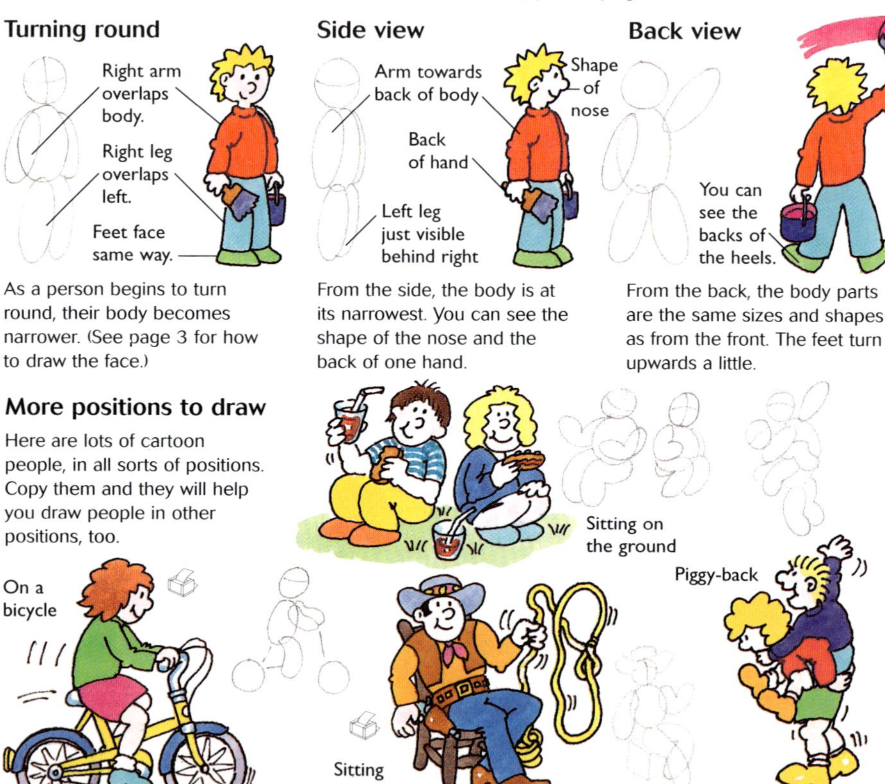

Turning round

As a person begins to turn round, their body becomes narrower. (See page 3 for how to draw the face.)

Side view

From the side, the body is at its narrowest. You can see the shape of the nose and the back of one hand.

Back view

From the back, the body parts are the same sizes and shapes as from the front. The feet turn upwards a little.

More positions to draw

Here are lots of cartoon people, in all sorts of positions. Copy them and they will help you draw people in other positions, too.

A bird's-eye view

A bird's-eye view can make an ordinary picture subject look quite different and dramatic. Try drawing this family group as seen from above.

The parts of the body nearer to you are bigger than those further away. Also, the bodies are shorter than if you were drawing them straight on from the front. This is called foreshortening.

Start by drawing a set of pencil lines fanning out from a point. Fit the people roughly in between them.

Heads look biggest as they are nearest.

Pencil lines help get the proportions of the people right.

Bodies get smaller the further away they are.

A worm's-eye view

Bodies get smaller the further away they are, and they are foreshortened.

A worm's-eye view is looking upwards from ground level. Draw another set of pencil lines starting from the top. This time, the legs and feet are biggest.

The head of the tallest person is the smallest.

Looking from the bottom, the feet are biggest.

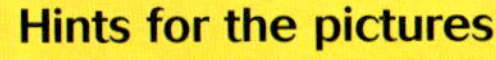

Hints for the pictures

Try to space the lines evenly. This means that all the people will get larger at the same rate.

Big people can slightly overlap the lines, and small people can fall within them.

The longer you draw the people, the more of a worm's-eye view the picture will become. This is also true for a bird's-eye view.

Moving pictures

Here, you can find out ways of drawing cartoon people walking, running, jumping and so on. Start with a stick or shape figure if it helps.

Walking and running

The right arm is in front when the left leg is forward.

Use this figure to help you get the body right.

When someone is walking briskly, they lean forward a little. There is always one foot on the ground.

Draw the figure just above ground level to show he is on the move.

Starting to run, the body leans forward even more. The elbows bend and move backwards and forwards.

Add a few curved lines to show fast movement.

Blobs of sweat flying off head

The faster someone is going, the more the body leans forward and the further the arms stretch.

Jumping

The more this leg bends, the higher the jump will be.

Running towards the jump...

Taking off...

In mid-flight...

Both feet come forward to hit the ground.

Landing from the jump

Falling over

These pictures show a stick person running along and tripping over. Copy them and then fill in the body shapes around the stick figures.

More movement

Here are some even more dramatic ways to show movement. You exaggerate certain things to give an impression of lots of speed or effort. You can write words on a picture to give extra impact.

Make the letters big and bold. You could do them in colour.

The person above is running to catch a bus. You could add words like ZOOM or WHIZZ, with an exclamation mark.

The hair and scarf of the skater on the left are streaming out behind her. This gives a sense of speed.

These figures look like they are running away. The dust clouds get smaller as they get further away.*

The figures are in the distance, so they are small. A curved line for the ground gives a feeling of space.

These silhouettes have long shadows to make it look like evening.

This is called perspective. There is more about it on page 13.

Drawing stereotypes

In cartoons, you can show what people do for a living by drawing a kind of caricature called a stereotype. People may be different shapes, have different expressions, move in different ways, wear different clothes and carry different tools, depending on what they do.

You normally recognize a stereotype from the shape of the body and the clothes. Here are a few you might like to try.

Getting started

If you like, draw stick figures or rounded shapes to help you get started on the figure. There is more about this on pages 4-5. Then you can work on the outline and clothes.

Can you see which characters some of these might belong to?

Chef

A stereotyped chef is jolly and round, with a big red face and a moustache.

No real burglar would wear this kind of outfit, but this is how they are generally drawn in cartoons.

The boxer is muscular and heavy, with a squashy nose and swollen ear. He wears big gloves and laced boots.

The ballerina is very slim and light on her feet. She stands on her toes.

Scenery and perspective

Scenery and backgrounds can add a lot of information about what is happening in your pictures. You need to keep the scenery quite simple, though, so that characters stand out against it.

Here, you can see how to get a sense of distance, or depth, into pictures. This is called drawing in perspective.

Tricks of perspective

The further away something is, the smaller it looks. The woman in this picture is drawn smaller than the burglar to make her look further away.

If you draw the woman level with the burglar, it will look like the picture above – she just looks like a tiny person. Draw her higher up to make her look more distant.

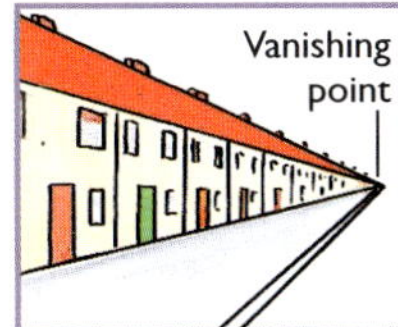

Parallel lines appear to get closer the further away they are. They seem to meet at a point on the horizon. This is called the vanishing point.

A high vanishing point makes it seem as if you are looking down on the picture. What do you think happens if you draw a low vanishing point?

A picture in perspective

Here is a picture in perspective. The woman is drawn smaller and further up than the burglar to make her look further away.

If the vanishing point falls outside your picture area, try sketching it in pencil as above. This helps to get all the lines properly in perspective. You can rub the lines out later.

Find out more about using perspective in your drawings at
www.sanford-artedventures.com/create/tech_1pt_perspective.html

Cartoon jokes

Cartoon jokes are often printed in newspapers and magazines. They may appear as a strip (see pages 16-17) or a single picture, called a single cartoon. The one on the right is a single cartoon.

Here you can find out what kind of jokes make good cartoons, what materials cartoonists use and some tips on drawing single cartoons yourself.

What makes a good single cartoon?

- A lot of information about what is happening and a lot of the humour in the picture itself
- A short caption
- A joke that is quick and easy to get.

The type of joke that makes a good single cartoon usually has the qualities shown above.

Ideas for jokes

It can be difficult to think up ideas for jokes on the spot. You might find it easier to think first of a theme or a situation. This may then suggest something funny to you.

Here are some common cartoon themes and some jokes based on them.

A desert island

This is one of the most common themes for single cartoon jokes.

A hospital

This joke has two common cartoon themes – hospitals and manhole covers.

Vampires

This is funny because it shows a monstrous creature doing something ordinary.

Materials you can use

The materials shown below are all you need to get started. They are not expensive to buy, and you may already have them anyway. If you like, though, you can buy some of the specialized materials shown on the rest of this page.

Pencils are marked to show how hard or soft they are. Experiment to find a type you like. Pencils range from 12B (very soft) to 12H (very hard).

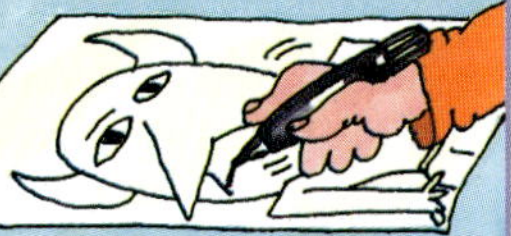

You can draw on good quality copier paper which is not too expensive.

Felt-tip pens do not smudge or blot. In time, though, you may find that the ink fades in sunlight. If you find it easier, sketch a drawing in pencil first and then go over it with a pen.

How professional cartoonists work

Single cartoons are usually drawn in black and white for printing in newspapers and magazines. Here are some of the materials that cartoonists use.

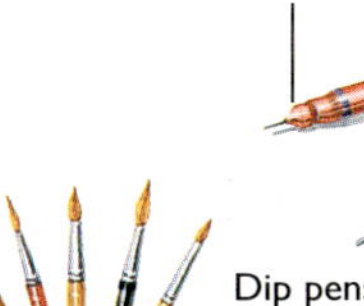

Drawing pens come with different thicknesses of nib. They draw a very even line.

Pencils: a cartoonist might use a medium pencil for outlines and a softer one for shading.

Dip pens and Indian ink: you can get different shapes and thicknesses of nib.

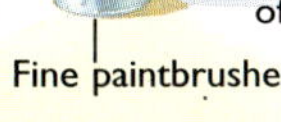

Fine paintbrushes

Art board can have different surfaces, from very smooth and shiny to quite rough and soft.

Cartridge paper takes pens, pencils or paint equally well.

Felt-tip pens

Fountain pens

Cartoons are usually printed quite small, but it is often easier for the cartoonist to draw them at a larger size. They can be reduced by computer for printing.

The cartoonist is told what the printed size will be. By drawing a diagonal line across a box that size, he or she can extend the box so that it is larger but still the same shape.

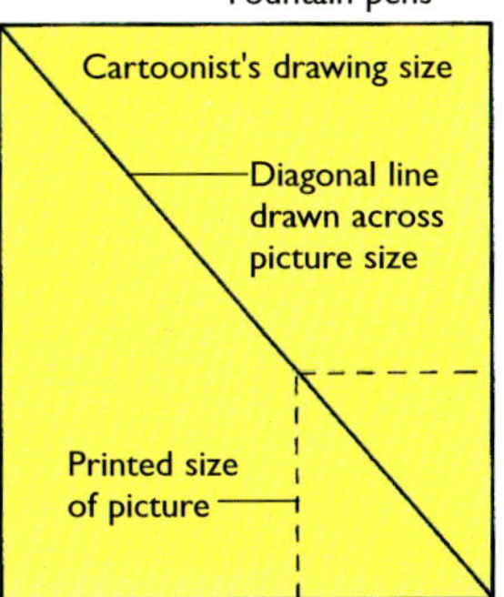

You can use different techniques and materials to colour cartoons. See how a professional cartoonist uses watercolour pencils at ***www.sanford-artedventures.com/create/tech_watercolor_pencil.html***

Short comic strips

A comic strip is like a joke told in more than one frame. As in a single cartoon, the joke needs to be visual. It can be like a short story with a punchline.

In comic strips, it can be hard to make characters look the same in each frame. To start with, only use one or two characters. Give them features that are easy to draw.

How to start

As with single cartoons. think of a theme first and make up a joke around it.

Close-ups varied with larger scenes

Divide the joke up into three or four stages. You can vary the sizes of the frames, and vary close-ups with larger scenes, to make the strip look more interesting.

Speech bubbles

You can put speech and thoughts in bubbles in the pictures. These can be different shapes. The shape of a bubble may suggest the way something is being said.

Put bubbles over background areas with no detail.

Keep the speech short or the strip gets complicated and the bubbles take up too much room. Make sure you allow room for bubbles when you sketch out the pictures.

It is best to do the lettering before you draw the bubble outline. Use a pen with a fine tip.

To get the letters the same height, draw parallel pencil lines and write the letters evenly in between them, as above. Then rub out the pencil lines. The letters are likely to be quite small, so it is best to use capital letters which are easier to read.

A finished comic strip

This strip is about a caveman and a dinosaur. The caveman is quite an easy character to repeat from frame to frame because of his simple features and clothing.

Speech bubble over the sky area

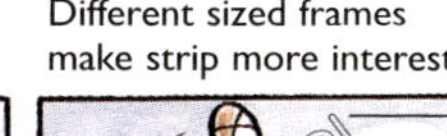

Different sized frames make strip more interesting

Sound effects make the strip more fun. As you read it you imagine the noises, so it is a little like watching a film.

Bright colours make the characters stand out. The background is paler.

A lot of the humour in a comic strip comes from the expressions on the characters' faces.

When positioning speech bubbles, remember that people read from left to right down the frame. They will read bubbles at the top before they read bubbles further down.

Borders for the strip

The borders round the frames can make a strip look neat and tidy or free and artistic. Here are some ideas for different borders you can try.

Freehand borders give a sketchy effect. To keep them straight, draw the lines in pencil with a ruler. Then go over them freehand in ink.

Paintbrush borders look good because the line varies slightly in thickness. You can get a straight line by using the method below.

Border round strip

Use a ruler and a pen with a slightly thicker tip than the one you used for the lettering. You can put the whole strip in a larger box.

Freehand borders are finished off without a ruler.

1. Place a ruler just below where you want to draw the line.
2. Hold the ruler down and run your fingers along it as you paint. (You may need to practise this.)

Long comic strips

You may have your own favourite comics. The stories in them are fun and easy to read because there is very little text and a lot of action in the pictures.

These two pages describe how a cartoon artist creates a comic strip to tell a story. Try making up your own comic strip in the same way.

Creating a comic strip

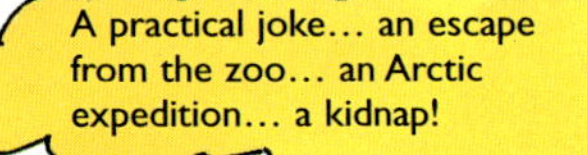

The first thing to do when creating a comic strip is to think of a plot. It needs to be funny or dramatic – or both! The plot needs an exciting finish.

The characters need strong personalities which will come across in the pictures. You can tell what the characters above are like just by looking at them.

Find out how to use special effects to add excitement to your pictures on pages 20-21.

The plot needs to be full of action to keep the reader interested. The story needs to move fast and something new must happen in each picture.

Writing a script

A script explains what is happening in each frame of the comic strip. It describes the scenery, what the characters are doing and saying and any sound effects. Some artists write their own scripts. Others illustrate scripts written by someone else.

The page of a comic is a fixed size so the story needs to be divided up into the right number of frames to fit on it.

SCRIPT: THE TESTTUBE AFFAIR
PAGE 1

Frame 1.
Scene: Room furnished with an iron bedstead. There is a small window. Terry is sitting tied to a chair, busy freeing himself.

Thought bubble: Whoever heard of a kidnapper who couldn't tie knots? I've been lucky.

Frame 2.
Scene: Sparsely-furnished room. There is a radio on the table. Two mean and grubby-looking kidnappers sit playing cards.

First kidnapper: Why do we always get the boring jobs?
Second kidnapper: Shuddup and listen!

Frame 3.
Close-up of radio blaring...

Drawing the strip

Here you can see how the script on the left (you can only see the first page) was made into a finished comic strip. It was drawn using a dip pen with a sprung nib. The nib gives a varying thickness of line depending on how hard it is pressed.

The story is mainly told in the pictures but there are bubbles for speech and thoughts.

Pressure on the nib gives a thick line.

Frame sizes are varied to make strip more interesting.

A line of text at the top can explain changes of scene or time lapses.

Some frames can be left without borders to add variety.

Light pressure on the nib gives a finer line.

Sound effects can help to tell the story.

Scenery can make the strip come to life.

Special effects

Special effects can make cartoons look exciting. Here are some ideas for how to add drama and atmosphere to your pictures. You can make them spooky, mysterious, shocking or scary. You can also find out how to add sound effects.

Sound effects

You can add sound effects by using words and shapes which suggest the sound. The most common ones are explosions, but there are lots of others you can use.

Jagged speech bubble suggests shock

Shadows and silhouettes

Using different lighting effects for night pictures can make them look creepy or mysterious. Here are some suggestions:

Silhouettes in a lighted window. These are made by people sitting in front of a source of light.

Huge shadow on wall

Silhouette of a castle in a thunderstorm

Scary effects

This picture uses the effect of a harmless tree that looks scary in the dark. You could try a similar picture using a hat and coat hanging up to look like a sinister person.

Two comic strips

These comic strips use some of the special effects described on these pages.

1

2

A comic strip to try

Here is a script for a comic strip involving special effects for you to try:

Frame 1. Silhouettes of people by a bonfire.

Frame 2. Boy dressed up as a ghost frightens them away.

Frame 3. Boy takes sheet off and is shocked to hear laughter coming from a spooky tree silhouette.

Sound effect: HO HO HO

Drawing animals

You can draw animals in a similar way to drawing people, by using simple shapes and lines and adding features.

Animals make good cartoons because you can use their natural characteristics, such as claws, tails, ears and so on to give them personality. Here are lots of animals to draw.

Cat

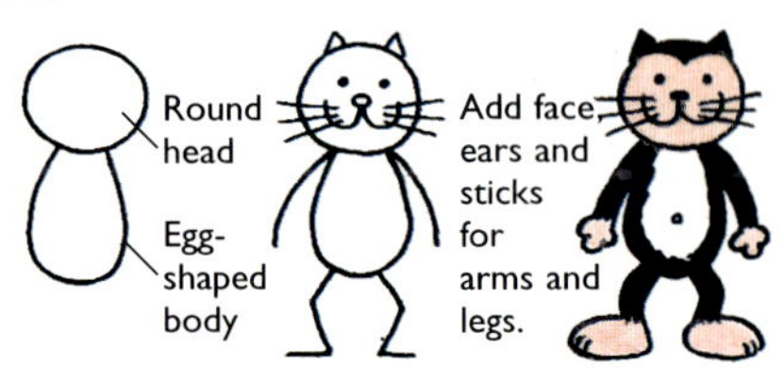

Dog

Mouse

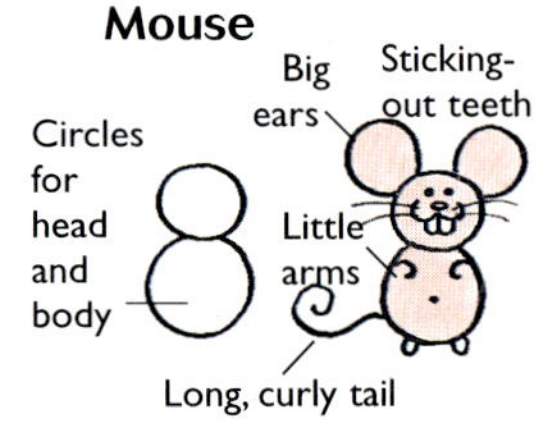

Bird

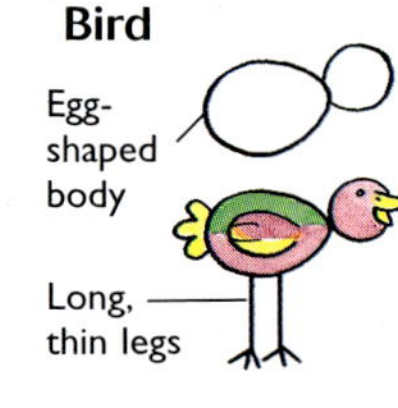

Pig

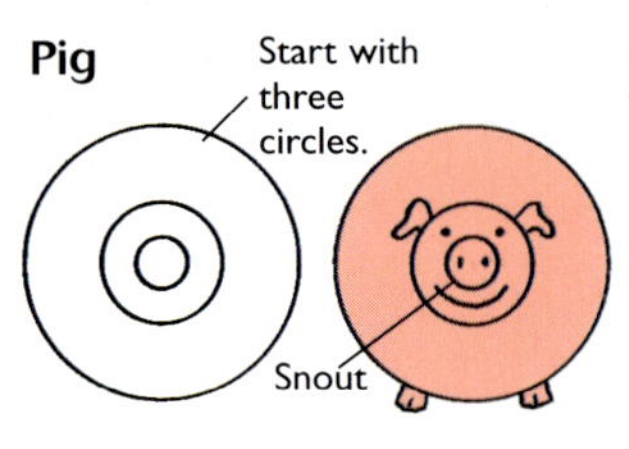

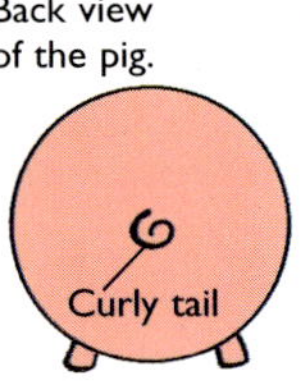

Giraffe

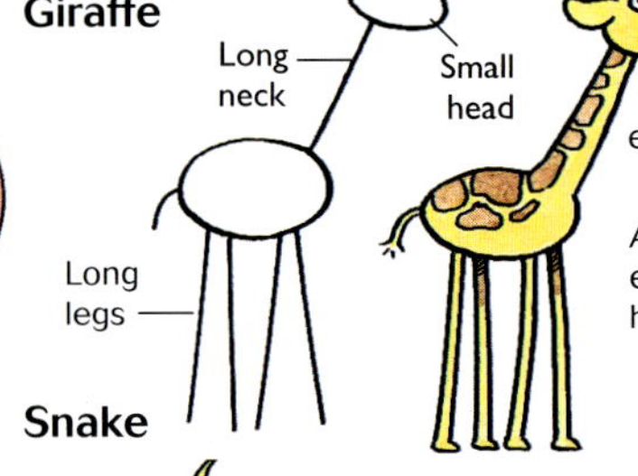

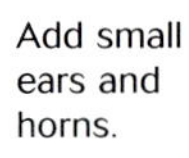

Elephant

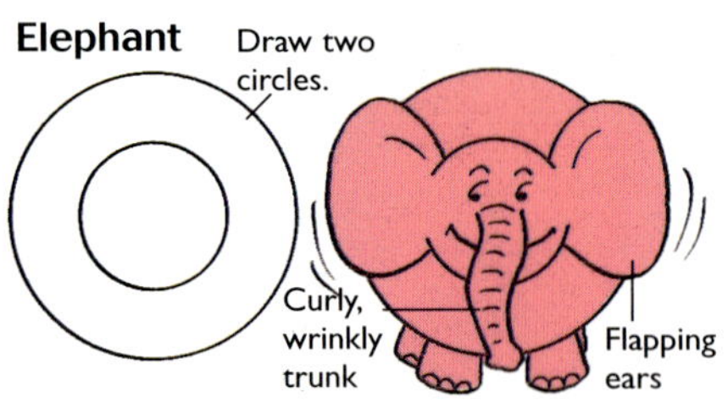

Snake

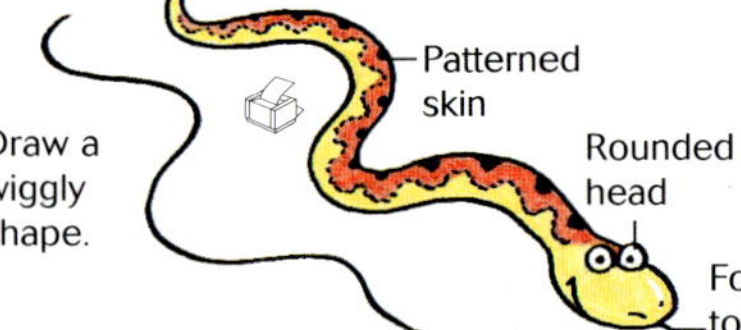

Internet links

For more information about drawing cartoons, go to the Usborne Quicklinks Web site at **www.usborne-quicklinks.com** where you'll find quick and easy access to the following recommended Web sites:

Draw and Color with Uncle Fred – Step-by-step instructions to help you draw and colour a dozen different cartoons.
www.unclefred.com

Cartoon Critters – More step-by-step instructions for drawing cartoon animals.
www.cartooncritters.com/learntodraw.htm

How to Draw with Slylock Fox – Lots more cartoon tutorials. You can also have drawing tips e-mailed to you each week.
www.slylockfox.com/how_draw.html

Dancing Bear – This site has tutorials for simple cartoons, and special tips for drawing details such as eyes.
www.dancing-bear.co.uk

Drawing Tricks – Try these drawing games yourself, then try inventing some similar ones for your friends.
www.cartooncorner.com/artsfolder/drawinggames/drawgames.html

Willing To Try – A few lines can turn into all kinds of things, with a little imagination.
www.willing-to-try.com

A History of Sequential Art – People have been telling stories in pictures for thousands of years. This site shows examples from cave paintings to Spiderman.
www.comic-art.com/history/history0.htm

Animation "How To" – If you are interested in animated cartoons, find out how they are made on this Cartoon Network site.
cartoonnetwork.com/doc/animation_primer/index.html
You can also go on a virtual tour of the Hanna-Barbera studios, where many famous cartoons were created.
cartoonnetwork.com/doc/hbtour/index.html

Yahooligans! Downloader – Comics and Animation – Links to over eighty galleries featuring famous cartoon characters.
www.yahooligans.com/Downloader/Pictures/Entertainment/Comics___Animation

Cartooning Tips – You'll find some useful advice here to help you experiment and practise your drawing.
www.teleport.com/~hsimante/hartext/cartoontips.html

All you Need to Know About Cartooning – This site offers more useful tips, including advice on what you can do if you want to have your cartoons published.
home3.inet.tele.dk/timslee/lesson.htm

Index

First published in 2001 by Usborne Publishing Ltd., 83-85 Saffron Hill, London EC1N 8RT, England. www.usborne.com
Copyright © 2001, 1987 Usborne Publishing Ltd. The name Usborne and the device are Trade Marks of Usborne Publishing Ltd. All rights reserved. No part of this publication may be reproduced, stored in a retrieval system or transmitted in any form or by any means, electronic, mechanical, photocopying, recording or otherwise, without the prior permission of the publisher. Printed in China.

Usborne Publishing are not responsible and do not accept liability, for the availability or content of any Web site other than our own, or for any exposure to harmful, offensive, or inaccurate material which may appear on the Web. Usborne Publishing will have no liability for any damage or loss caused by viruses that may be downloaded as a result of browsing the sites we recommend. Usborne downloadable pictures are the copyright of Usborne Publishing Ltd and may not be reproduced in print or in electronic form for any commercial or profit-related purpose.